A
VERY
CORGI
Christmas

For my lovely mum — S.H.
For Ruby xx — L.S.

SIMON & SCHUSTER
First published in Great Britain in 2018 by Simon & Schuster UK Ltd
1st Floor, 222 Gray's Inn Road, London, WC1X 8HB • A CBS Company
Text copyright © 2018 Sam Hay • Illustrations copyright © 2018 Loretta Schauer
The right of Sam Hay to be identified as the author and Loretta Schauer as the illustrator
of this work has been asserted by them in accordance with the Copyright, Designs and
Patents Act, 1988 • All rights reserved, including the right of reproduction in whole
or in part in any form • A CIP catalogue record for this book is available from
the British Library upon request.
978-1-4711-7775-0 (PB) • 978-1-4711-7777-4 (eBook)
Printed in China • 10 9 8 7 6 5 4 3 2 1

A VERY CORGI Christmas

Sam Hay & Loretta Schauer

SIMON & SCHUSTER

London   New York   Sydney   Toronto   New Delhi

It was Christmas Eve. And Buckingham Palace was a flurry of activity.

BEEP

BEEP
BEEP

There were comings and goings,

to-ings and fro-ings,

and people here, there and everywhere.

The royal corgis were not amused.

"Too much fuss!"

"Too much chatter!"

"Too much bother!"

But one young corgi was excited.
Belle loved all the Christmas preparations . . .

a little too much!

"Stop getting in the way!" the older dogs barked
at her. "Christmas is NOT for corgis!"

Belle crept off
to her basket.

"I wish Christmas WAS for corgis," she thought.
"It looks such fun."

Just then, a snowflake drifted
in from the open window and
landed on her nose. It smelt —

MAGICAL!

In the distance she could see hundreds of bright,
twinkling lights. They looked —

DAZZLING!

And on the streets there were so many
people AND dogs, hustling and bustling.
It sounded —

EXCITING!

"Everyone out there seems to be
enjoying Christmas," Belle thought,
"so perhaps that's where I should go!"

And she slipped through an open door . . .

into the back of a van!

"Oh!" thought Belle.
"This really IS exciting."

VROOOOOOM!

When the van stopped, the doors opened and Belle tumbled out.

She blinked and gasped.
The world outside the palace
was bright. A bit too bright.

And busy. So busy!

And loud. Very loud!

FAR TOO LOUD!

"Hello," said a kind voice. "Are you lost?"

Belle looked up into a warm, furry face with a smudgy nose and twinkly, crinkly eyes.

"I'm Pip," said the dog.

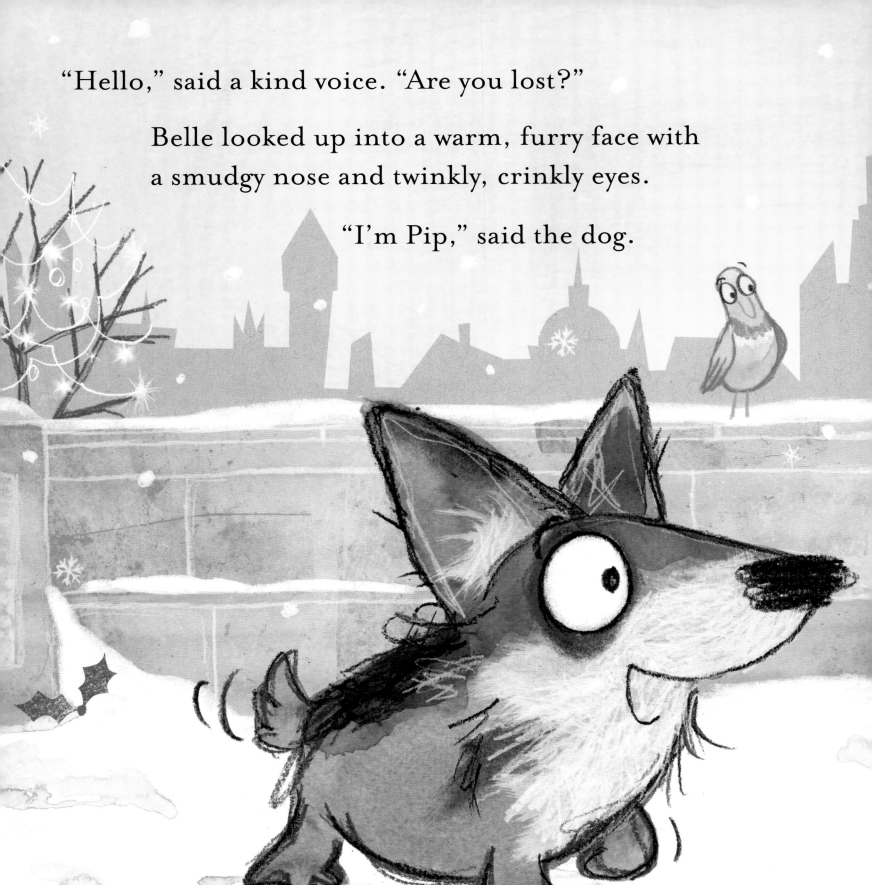

"I'm Belle," said Belle. "And I'm not sure I like it here."

"Really? But this is London AND it's Christmas, so it's double the fun! I'll show you."

They hitched a ride,

and flew in the sky.

They saw some tick-tock places,

and found some
snuggly spaces.

Pip made everything sparkly and special.

"I'm staying here with you forever!" Belle declared. "That would be lovely," Pip smiled. "But won't your family be worried?"

Belle thought about home . . . about her kind, caring family and the cosy corgi cuddles at night . . .

Pip was right.

They WOULD be worried.

But getting back into Buckingham Palace wasn't going to be easy.

"You see, I'm not supposed to be outside," Belle explained.

"Don't worry," said Pip, with a wink. "Where there's a waggy tail, there's a way!"

First, they tried climbing the walls . . . with a bit of help from Pip's pals.

Next, they tried sneaking in with the soldiers.

HALT!

Nothing worked. But Belle had one last idea . . .

It involved something that she
had never EVER tried before.

LITTER BIN RAIDING!

Then they hid in the shadows, until a long,
black car drove up to the palace gates and . . .

WOOF! Belle and Pip jumped out!

On the number plate: ROYAL 1

They waggled their flags and tooted and
hooted and made a humongous hullaballoo.

Then one of the windows opened . . .

"It's BELLE!" said a voice from inside the car. "And who's that other dog with her? Let's take them inside."

"Come on, Pip!" Belle called. "I can't wait for you to meet my family!"

But Pip had gone.

Everyone was so happy to see Belle
back at Buckingham Palace.

"Perhaps Christmas CAN
be for corgis!" they woofed.

But Belle couldn't stop thinking about Pip.

So she looked up into the starry
sky and made a wish . . .

It was Christmas morning. And Buckingham Palace
was a flurry of activity. There were treats and gifts
and wonderful surprises.

But the biggest and most
wonderful surprise of all
was for Belle.

"Pip!"

"Merry Christmas, Belle."

Which just goes to show,
sometimes wishes do come true.